Immortaland

The Greatest Fantasy Kingdom To Exist And That Will Ever Exist

By Blaine Hart

Introduction

Sit down, grab some popcorn, and prepare to have your mind blown as you are guided through the greatest fantasy kingdom to exist and that will ever exist!

The Fantasy Kingdom: Immortaland

And so it was that after thirty years of adventuring, leveling, learning, and becoming even more powerful, the mighty hero was able to manipulate time, open a portal, slay the guardian, defeat the evil king, and claim the all mighty book of knowledge for his own. After several more decades of diligent study, research, and praying, he was finally strong enough, pure enough, powerful enough and wise enough to create his very own magical kingdom with unlimited power. He named this kingdom IMMORTALAND, and he lived there forever more, happy as anyone could ever hope to be, making his kingdom stronger and better every chance he got! Immortaland has now gone exponential and is a mighty bastion of goodness that ensures the abundant existence of all that is good throughout all of space and time.

You say the magic words: "Immortaland, Immortaland, Immortaland"

     You suddenly find yourself in a beautiful field filled with bright green grass and beautiful flowers of all descriptions. Blue, orange, red, and yellow butterflies flap in the warm breeze and the two suns are bright among puffy white clouds. The sky is a beautiful shade of blue. Looking down, you see yourself in a diamond circle, easily five feet wide. The gems sparkle under the noon day suns and in the golden road in which they are embedded.

Behind you, the golden road ends abruptly at the entrance to a beach paradise overflowing with yellow sand. Waves of pure clean water splash merrily against the sandy shore, inviting you to jump in and take a swim. Where the golden road turns into yellow sand, stand two beautiful smiling women. One has long flowing blonde hair and is wearing a tight red bikini, while the other has fiery red hair tied back in a diamond pony tail, sporting a yellow bikini studded with rubies. The red head, named Sandra, blows you a kiss, while the blonde, named Beverlyn, beckons for you to come and join them on the beach. You wave to them and then run into their welcoming embrace, giving each a passionate kiss on the lips. With a tinge of regret you tell them "Have some fun without me for a bit, I will be back shortly."

The look of sadness on their faces and their disappointed whimpering is too much to bear, so you raise your fist in the air, calling upon the magical powers that are everywhere in this land, and suddenly a clone of yourself appears, complete with golden armor and crown. Your clone gives you a knowing wink and then grabs each woman by the hand and starts heading for the beach. "Come on ladies, you can help me get out of this armor." The women giggle as the trio run to the beach.

Turning around, you see the golden brick road ending at the base of a massive fairy tale castle of diamond and pure white marble. There are four massive towers on each corner of the castle, and a great tower in the center, which reaches high into the puffy white clouds.

The great tower is enchanted with an un-breakable magical shield of power that extends one-hundred miles in all directions, including above and underneath the massive island. Each of the diamond and white marble corner towers is capped with turrets of solid gold that sparkle under the life giving suns. Each tower is equipped with their own unique set of deadly weapons, guardians, traps, enchantments, and defenses to keep the realm safe.

At the base of the castle are a magnificent assortment of rose bushes, orange trees, raspberry bushes, apple trees, and all sorts of other flowers, herbs, and fruit trees. All of the fruits and flowers are in full bloom, and stay that way throughout the years by the powerful magic emanating from the castle itself.

You can hear songbirds chirping merrily and can see many others flying through the air or sitting in the trees, their beauty a joy to behold. The birds here are magical, and have the effect of making you feel healthy and happy just by watching them and listening to their beautiful songs. This is also a favorite place for pets, animals, and magical creatures of the realm to get together and play in the bountiful gardens that surround the castle.

Looking around, you can see several great heroes from legends, stories, and from famous video games strolling along and looking quite heroic. You teleport over to them, slapping them a high five! You then recount some stories of your epic adventures together, bringing smiles all around. After a few fond memories you say goodbye, knowing that if any trouble should arise, that these heroes and all the other heroes located throughout Immortaland will fight to the death for your cause.

Ahead of you, the golden road ends at a large diamond door in the center of the castle. A fabulous sun of yellow diamonds decorates the center of the door, shining brightly, and emitting another, more powerful shield that protects everything within 100 feet of the castle.

Below the sun is a golden doorknob over a magically glowing lock. Above the door is a powerful magical ward placed there by ten demi-gods and twenty masterful wizards. This powerful ward of protection will prevent evil from entering the castle, as well as preventing anyone or anything which intends to do harm to Immortaland or its occupants from entering or even getting within three hundred feet of the castle in all directions.

If anything not an ally of Immortaland does get close, the magical ward will disintegrate them into atoms and then scatter those atoms throughout space and time or capture them for rehabilitation.

The heroes of Immortaland all have keys to the door, and you do not need a key because you can teleport anywhere in Immortaland at will, with ultimate power to do as you please. Next to the door is a large ruby, which can be pressed to produce a melodic chime that will summon the great genie to see who is there.

Turning around, you see Sandra and Beverlyn, standing at the entrance to the beach with your well muscled clone, warm smiles on all their faces. You run over to them, enjoying the feel of the sand under your feet and the sun on your face. There are many women on the beach along with quite a few heroes. They are sun tanning, swimming, playing games, and talking to each other. You smile bright, knowing that everyone here and in this entire realm are all here for your enjoyment.

You become one with your clone, and then put your arms around both girls, giving Beverlyn a long french kiss while Sandra looks on jealously. When you finally pull away, you notice that Beverlyn's lips are even more luscious and beautiful than before. This is another great power you possess, the ability to make anyone better looking and full of energy just by willing it or kissing them.

It's not long before a crowd of beautiful heroines and ladies is surrounding you, giving you compliments, and fawning over your every move. You give them all the attention they deserve, and then with a wave you stroll down the beach towards the water.

The waves splash merrily against the shore, and you notice many colorful shells on the beach along with various exotic fish that swim in the crystal clear water. Three hundred feet ahead of you, sprouting twenty feet high out of the sea, is a mesmerizing solid crystal wall that extends hundreds of feet into the air. The top of the wall is seventy feet wide and covered in a long line of crystal turrets, allowing for defenders to easily fight here at a major advantage.

This mighty unbreakable crystal wall encircles the whole main island of Immortaland and glitters under the suns during the day and glows brightly at night. At a seconds notice, the entire wall can be lowered into the ocean, to allow the warships to get out, or it can be raised up at incredible speed to encircle the land and smash anything in its way.

Suddenly, several silver colored fish fly high out of the water and then splash back down into the sparkling blue ocean, as a magnificent eight foot long sea turtle surfs a large wave onto shore next to you. The giant turtle has a rainbow colored shell that sparkles red, gold, silver, blue, yellow, and orange. He has a long silver head and golden flippers. His name is "Algarion the Defender", and he is a mighty protector of Immortaland. He can be ridden all around the island, and even deep out to sea if need be. He also emits a magical air bubble around him that allows anyone riding him to breathe underwater while suffering no ill effects from water pressure if deep under the ocean.

Many of the local heroes love to go explore the deep underwater reefs with him, or visit the underwater village of mermaids and mermen that help protect the land. Algarion the Defender is much more than he appears, however, he is also one of the most powerful guardians of the realm, and totally loyal to you.

If trouble should arise, he can magically transform himself into a five hundred foot tall rainbow dragon, with scales of every color under the sun. Just the sight of him is enough to scare away most enemies, and blind others. He has the powers and abilities of every dragon ever thought about or conceived of throughout all of space and time, and he cannot be killed. His teeth and claws can puncture anything, and you can teleport with him to anyplace in the universe. Algarion also has three twin brothers just as powerful as he, who take turns guarding Immortaland while the others spend their time searching distant realms for items, resources, or defenders to make Immortaland even more powerful. If trouble should arise, they can always teleport back to Immortaland instantly.

You pat Algarion the Defender on the head, and suddenly, feeling a surge of power, you jump fifty feet into the air towards the crystal wall, do six front flips, and then dive into the deep sea. The water is cool and refreshing, and the bottom of the sea is covered in a multitude of beautiful plants, corals, and shells.

You swim powerfully to the crystal ramp at the base of the wall and jump on it. A set of stairs leads to the top of the wall and one of the many crystal turrets that line the top it. You fly to the top, raise your hands in the air, spread them wide, look up at the suns, and absorb incredible amounts of energy and power.

The main sun here is a powerful magical artifact that harnesses the power of all the other suns in existence, and then uses that energy to empower Immortaland and all who live there.

The other sun glows red and grants incredible luck and health from its powerful blaze. Once a week the red sun will start to glow green, granting increased wisdom and incredible foresight into the future for anyone in the realm.

You float there in the air, absorbing even more power from the two suns, allowing yourself to glow a bright yellow. You then summon your twenty foot long angelic wings of ultimate power and flex them to full length, relishing in the power of it all. When fully satisfied, you fly high into the sky, then free fall towards the deepest end of the ocean, doing multiple backflips before landing a perfect dive into the deep sea. The water feels great and you proceed to swim several times around the island, checking on several secret underground caves where various high level experiments are being performed.

You then swim towards shore, your ripped muscles propelling you along at great speed. You body surf a large wave onto shore and are greeted by an assortment of heroes and heroines. You take the time to talk to each one of them, addressing their concerns or enjoying their praise and compliments. After everyone has had their time with you, you wave your hand and smile as you are suddenly clad in fabulous silks with a large crown of ultimate power on your head. You walk leisurely across the beach, admiring the scantily clad women one last time as you walk back onto the golden road.

Whistling a merry tune, you decide to levitate for a bit over the golden road while taking in deep breaths of the pure fresh air. You follow the road through a field of flowers and fairies, over the glowing teleport circle, and to the gold and diamond doors of the castle itself. You clap your hands and the door swings open before you. There is a musical chime as you enter, filling you with a sense of well being. You find yourself in a huge and lavishly decorated great hall. In each corner of the hall there are one hundred foot high emerald statues of mighty wizards holding a staff of immense power in one hand, and a mighty book of spells in the other.

From the staffs of each wizard bursts a magical white fire that floods the whole room with light. Any invader to this hall will find that the wizards have come to life to blast them to pieces, turn them into a toad, or teleport them somewhere they really don't want to be.

On the northern wall hang one hundred and fifty million of the greatest weapons, armor, and magic items ever used by legendary heroes, demi -gods, and video game characters throughout all of space and time. These weapons and armaments are secured to the wall by magical bands of power and may only be taken off the wall by an ally of Immortaland.

At your feet you notice a gemstone path that goes for several hundred yards and then through another circular teleporter made from rubies and the blood of a powerful red dragon to a golden door thirty feet high and covered in magical glowing healing runes. The teleporter catches your eye, the six inch high red flames beckoning you to enter. On either side of the gemstone pathway you see magnificent statues of fabulous beasts, glorious heroes, and mighty demi-gods.

To your left you notice that the whole western half of the room is a magnificent garden paradise, with a fabulous golden pool in the center of it all. A sparkling emerald path leads to the outside edge of the pool. The pool itself is fifty feet deep and easily three hundred feet wide. Around the edge of the pool are four fifty foot high white marble statues of muscular unicorns, with their front legs in the air and water spouting in great gouts from their crystal horns to splash down all about the pool.

As the water hits the pool, there is a small explosion of rainbow colored light that several small fairies like to dance around. On the outside edge of the pool, there are all sorts of flowers in full bloom, and a beautiful grass path that winds through the garden. In several clearings there are marble benches, fabulous silk couches, as well as three brilliantly fashioned sapphire gazebos.

You follow the grass path to the edge of the pool and jump in, admiring the many beautiful fish swimming in the water. You swim down deep to the bottom of the pool and notice many open sacks of gold, chests overflowing with gems, fabulous shells, and several glowing magical weapons. You grab an unusually large sack of gold and swim back up to the surface with it, and then hop out of the pool. With a flourish you toss the coins back into the pool, wishing for great wealth and love. The unicorns glow brightly, shooting out multi-colored sparks as your wish is granted.

You spend several more hours here relaxing, swimming, and enjoying the sweet smells, pleasant noises, and beautiful plant life. You walk over to a nearby flowered clearing and look up, gazing at the castles ceiling. It is one thousand feet high and is a huge magical screen that looks like an ever shifting stained glass window when it is not being actively used. By shouting the command word: "travel time," the ceiling becomes a massive 3d picture of anything or anyplace in the whole universe.

By shouting "go", you will be magically transported to your desired location, with your powers and abilities only limited by your imagination. There are over a million fail safe mechanisms in place to ensure ultimate safety and a great time while visiting the many alternate realities that exist.

While in these realms, you may do any great deed you wish, and you may also move forward and backward in time at will. The place pictured does not even have to be real; you can create your own fantastical place to venture forth to. You can return at any time just by saying "Immortaland" three times.

In the south western corner of this room is a large golden door that is thirty feet high and decorated with carvings of great heroes. This door leads to the heroes' tower, where all the great heroes, real or imagined, from millions of different universes, dwell in total luxury. They are allowed full access to Immortaland, and in return are sworn to protect it with their lives.

The heroes are a lively bunch and it is always fun to visit them. You clap your hands and suddenly you are dressed in golden armor, with a bright red flowing cape of light, a large golden crown, and a magical sword of unrivaled power. You stride over to the door and throw it open, striding up a magnificent diamond stairwell, well lit with magical, smokeless torches floating near the ceiling.

Once up the stairs and through another mighty protective door, you find yourself in the heroes' tower. The main living room is over three thousand yards wide and filled with fireplaces, tables, chairs, full weapon racks, workout equipment, and anything a hero could ever want or request. In the center of the room is a magical glowing teleporter, which can be used to transport a hero or heroine to their own personal kingdom, or anywhere else in Immortaland.

As a reward for protecting Immortaland for all eternity, each hero is given a kingdom with a lavish castle, shrunk through magic to fit inside of Immortaland at the size of a grain of sand, and kept hidden inside an invisible and unbreakable orb of magic in the treasure chamber. The kingdoms of the heroes and heroines are similar to Immortaland itself; however each is free to modify it to their own tastes and desires.

In the center of this room is a beautiful octagon arena, made of pure magic. The heroes take turns fighting in the arena, sharpening their skills, and allowing the arena to absorb some of their power while simultaneously making them more powerful.

You walk into the arena which is pulsating with unbelievable amounts of heroic energy, spread your hands wide, and absorb the power and battle splendor that has accumulated here since your last visit. Lightning bursts from every corner of the arena as you absorb it all. Shouting out a powerful war cry "Immortaland!" that echoes throughout the kingdom, you proceed to high five all the other adventurers you see here, and kissing a few of the hot heroines. After visiting some of your favorite heroes, heroines, kings and queens in their home castles, you head down the staircase and back into the main hall.

Whistling a merry tune, you float along the great hall, heading for the eastern part of the massive chamber. With just a thought, you suddenly sprout magnificent golden wings and spread them wide.

You float along a beautiful path of sparkling rubies that leads you to a massive diamond fireplace in the middle of the eastern wall. It is easily twenty feet high and thirty feet long. Inside the fireplace burns a powerful magical fire that never goes out, always burning fiercely, and emanating from it a pure, holy energy.

You walk up to the fireplace, noticing that the flames do not burn, and walk in. You instantly feel all your negativity melting away in the holy fire, and you relish in the wholesome feeling that permeates every fiber of your being. You rejoice in the heavenly feeling that overcomes you and smile. You will now have nothing but happy and positive thoughts for the next week. After several minutes of pure ecstasy, you walk out, feeling pure and at peace with the universe.

Looking around the fireplace, you notice that the outside edges consist of fabulous carvings of angels and magical symbols of good. On the diamond fireplace mantel are some of the finest treasures ever taken by brave fantasy adventurers from fearsome foes. There are magic wands, powerful potions, magic gems, bags of unending gold, works of art, weapons, and many other magical items. A favorite is a magically enchanted silver helm. It is covered in brightly glowing runes of power, that when placed on the head, it gives the wearer incredible powers of the mind, including telepathy, increased intelligence, wisdom, and foresight.

You walk over to the fireplace and put on the magnificently crafted helm. You suddenly feel brilliant, and with a click something goes off in your head "Ahhh, so that is the secret of life." you whisper to yourself chuckling.

Looking up, fifty feet over the fireplace mantelpiece, is a twenty foot by twenty foot sun made of small yellow, red, and orange gemstones that swirl around hypnotically. Fabulous paintings and tapestry's of Kings and famous battles cover the rest of the wall.

Around the fireplace are several magnificent couches and chairs. On one end table there lies a golden pitcher that holds the sweetest of wines known in the universe. The pitcher is enchanted so that it is always full, and the wine never gives a hang over or makes you too drunk.

There is also a large oak table here, with fifty chairs around it. In the center of the table is a crystal sphere, which, when touched, can produce a feast of the best food available in the universe, perfectly prepared, complete with jeweled dinnerware fit for an emperor. Another touch to the crystal can cause it all to disappear.

In the southeastern corner of this room is a ten foot tall door made of pure ruby. This door leads to the striking tower. Inside this tower is a magical ruby the size of a mighty Oak tree that can focus Immortaland's power to strike a devastating blow against its enemies. You walk over to a red couch of soft silk and lie down, looking into the flames of the fire and then the swirling flames of the sun above the mantel. After several minutes of daydreaming, you clap your hands and shout "Genie", and suddenly a beautiful woman appears in a puff of white smoke. She is wearing a pink bikini, and no top. She has long blonde hair streaked with black, a gorgeous face, a magnificent pair of tits, an unbelievable ass, and sparkling blue eyes. "Yes master" she states in a sultry voice.

"Bring me five women from around the realm who want to play." you command. She suddenly disappears, and one second later appears in a puff of white smoke with five gorgeous women. You stare at the beautiful women and they smile back at you. You break out the wine and serve it in the finest crystal glasses.

After several hours of play time, the genie and the women all go back to what they where doing before, all of them now even more beautiful and filled with energy. With a large grin on your face and a sense that all is well in the world, you walk over to the ruby door.

You find yourself in a room made of war ruby. War ruby consists of rubies that have been charged with the power of various different suns and power sources over thousands of years on a top secret planet. It is mainly used for blasting your enemies into atoms.

The main feature of this room is a massive war ruby shaped like a huge cannon that fills most of the chamber, with the barrel going through a large hole in the ceiling ten thousand feet in the air. This room is magically designed to focus an unbelievable amount of power and then send it out in a blast of ultimate energy power to obliterate your enemies.

There is a large monitor near the entrance of this room which can lock onto anyone or anything in the universe. Once a target has been picked, you simply have to press the large ruby button next to the monitor to blast it to smithereens. Of course, there are various limitations on what can and cannot be blasted by this ultimate weapon, so great care is always used when employing it. You pat the cannon, shivering with the raw power contained there, and then snap your fingers, stating "Throne Room."

You suddenly find yourself high in the sky, standing in the middle of an ever shifting circle of emeralds, sapphires, and diamonds, in the top most room of the great central tower. The teleporter you are standing in has the power to teleport you anywhere in the castle, its surrounding lands, as well as any other place in space and time. You smile and look around, admiring the mighty Throne Room.

The ceiling in this room is one hundred thousand feet high, and is made of enchanted diamond, save for a five foot wide circle in the center of the ceiling that is open to the sky. The walls, ceiling, and floor are covered with powerful magical glowing sigils of protection, making anyone in this room safe from all harm from any source. The power of this room is legendary to all who know of it, and many powerful beings would pay heed to the things that go on in here if they could.

The walls are pure enchanted diamond and they glow with a holy radiance. In the center of the chamber is a magnificent table made of pure platinum and perfectly round. There are eight chairs around the table, each made of a rare wood and covered in magical inscriptions that increase brain power, decision making ability, and overall strength. The chairs are padded with green silk, and many mighty heroes and kings have adorned them.

In the center of the table is a large, golden colored, multifaceted crystal orb ten feet wide. This crystal is a combination of one thousand of the most powerful magical gemstones ever created in all of eternity. They where fused together into this one ultimate crystal by a team of the best scientists, wizards, and demi-gods to ever exist on all of the different planes and dimensions of existence.

The mighty orb of power is aligned in the center of the throne room and in the center of the platinum table right under the opening in the ceiling. The whole room glows with the barely contained golden power that dwells within the orb, which has the ability to take any firmly stated desire or wish, amplify it a million times over, and then make it a reality.

This all powerful gem has full access to the great computer in the room of knowledge, and has the abilities of an all seeing, all powerful, crystal ball, able to see a clear picture of anything, anywhere in all the universes. If desired, the user can cast mighty spells directly onto any pictured area. It is also possible to see the future while gazing deep into the gem, although this tends to cost a lot of energy the further into the future you go.

You walk over and touch the ultimate orb, shivering with the power, and picturing yourself. You see yourself appear in the gem, strong and vibrant. You bring the picture in closer, and then cast a powerful spell of healing and strength. You smile as all your injuries heal and your body becomes fully energized, while brilliant sparkles surround you.

You are strong and feeling glad to be alive. You then cast another mighty spell, and a powerful aura of luck surrounds you. You then focus on wealth and love being attracted to you like a magnet, coming quickly and easily. The universe then bends to your will.

Raising your hands high and then touching the orb again, you summon all the power of Immortaland, and cast a permanence spell, making all the spells just cast a reality. Your body shimmers brightly, and you now feel unstoppable, leading a path to greatness, happiness, and unending joy.

You smile brightly, then summon Genie, and give her a long French kiss. Looking at the northern part of the room, you see a massive throne of gold, gems, and diamonds that glow brightly. It is covered in the most powerful protective symbols in the universe, and the throne itself has been blessed by ten of the holiest demi-gods and one thousand of the holiest priests ever to exist. Anyone seated upon this throne is safe from harm from any source, and any negative energy that has been directed toward them will be reflected away harmlessly.

You walk up to the throne and take a seat. You feel magnificent, a holy aura surrounds you, and you can feel all your negative thoughts and influences being repelled from you with enormous force.

While on this throne you can execute any order or decision that needs to be done in order for you to have ultimate success. You can easily communicate with all the inhabitants of Immortaland instantly while seated on the throne.

Also, while seated on the throne, you are blessed with the knowledge of the best course of action to take in any given situation for the greater good. After several minutes you have a clear plan in your head of exactly what to do in the next month in order to be performing at peak efficiency and improving the realm at optimum speed. Standing up, you flex your muscles, feeling great.

You then walk over to a chair at the platinum center table and take a seat. You smile then state "I want incredible wealth and happiness for myself and my allies." you state firmly, and then touch the ultimate gem of power. The orb pulsates with power and takes your wish, amplifies it a million fold, and then an explosion of golden light bursts from the top of the gem and out the hole in the ceiling to the universe for epic fulfillment. You smile in satisfaction, knowing that this goal will become a reality shortly in one way or another. You glow powerfully as you walk over to the teleport circle and state in a powerful voice: "Great Hall."

There is a flash and then you find yourself in the great hall, standing in the ruby circle. Directly ahead of you is a massive door of pure glowing healing energy. It is covered with multi-colored magical symbols of healing that shine brightly. Walking up to the door, you press your right hand against it. There is a flash as the door disappears, along with all your aches and pains. Walking inside, you find yourself in a large chamber with a ceiling that is thousands of feet high and made of pure healing crystals which glow brightly.

The circular walls are covered in emeralds, sapphires, rubies, diamonds, golden healing runes, silver healing runes, and multi-colored balls that glow brightly with pure healing energy. The floor is made up of a sheet of pure healing energy that has been crystallized through the work of many priests, wizards, scientists, and demi-gods. In the center of the room is a twenty foot by twenty foot bed with blue silk sheets that shimmer with healing energy. The bed is covered in beautiful pillows and fragrant flower petals, which exude a strong sense of warmth and comfort. Around the bed are twenty large and magical flowered plants which emit the perfect blend of healing vibrations to accelerate healing of the body and mind.

When on this bed, all of your mental and physical ailments are instantly cured. You run over and jump onto the bed, and all your injuries and worries instantly melt away. You lie down on the bed, instantly feeling relaxed as the surrounding crystals and plants glow brightly with powerful healing energy. You feel great and at one with the universe. The past is rosy, and the future is glorious.

After a few hours of feeling just incredible, you leave the magical healing chamber fully rested and head back into the great hall. You admire the wizards in the corners and the beautiful statues that are scattered throughout the hall. You then snap your fingers and find yourself in the brightly glowing red circle in the center of the hall. "Room of Luck!" you state with a grin.

In an instant you are transported deep into the heart of Immortaland, a magical chamber located one mile underneath the great hall. The room of luck is a sealed chamber, thirty feet wide and twenty feet tall. The floor is made of glowing yellow powerstone, which naturally enhances anyone's luck just by being around it. In the center of the room is a fabulous giant star that shimmers and pulses with waves of pure lucky energy.

It is the most powerful lucky artifact in existence, and it is made of concentrated yellow and green powerstone. Just by touching it, you will be granted good fortune for the next ten years. Underneath the lucky artifact is a trapdoor that leads down to the kingdoms treasure chamber. Only you, the lord of Immortaland, can access this trapdoor, and may do so just by snapping your fingers and using mental focus.

Anyone else who attempts to access the treasure chamber will find that the room isn't so lucky for them. The lucky artifact will come alive with energy and vaporize them where they stand.

You walk up to the glowing star, admiring the hundreds of different colors swirling on its surface. Touching it, you feel a powerful jolt of energy flow through you, increasing your luck a thousand fold and sending a tingle down your spine. The powerstone glows brightly around you, and you absorb all of the luck as it courses through your body.

You spend several minutes here, just taking it all in. You then snap your fingers and picture the statue moving to your left. It slides over easily, revealing a titanium steel trap door underneath it with one hundred locks.

Each lock is magically trapped and enchanted to destroy any unauthorized trespasser. You snap your fingers again, and one hundred keys appear from their secret hiding spots about Immortaland and turn in the locks. The trap door opens, revealing a glowing orange staircase that leads down to the treasure chamber.

Walking down the stairs several hundred feet, you find yourself in a magnificent treasure chamber five square miles wide and one hundred ten thousand feet high. On the western wall are hundreds of thousands of treasure chests filled to the brim with the most valuable materials and objects in all the known universes. Some chests hold diamonds, others gold, others are filled with silver coins, others hold gems, while many others hold magical items and all sorts of fabulous jewelry. Each chest is also magically enchanted to be able to hold massive quantities of material.

The eastern wall is covered in magical one way portals where treasure can come through from all around the known universes to collect here. There are several hundred magical pixies and dragons here with great magic power that organize the treasure, as well as guard it with their lives. The floor itself is covered in golden, silver, and platinum coins, gems, great pieces of art, magical spell books, magical items, and the most valuable of weapons and armor.

Incredibly beautiful works of art hang on the walls or stand on magnificent pedestals. This mighty treasure chamber holds at least ten of each magical item or treasure ever thought of throughout all of space and time that is of beneficial use to Immortaland. You stare in awe at the unimaginable wealth Immortaland has accumulated over the years with the help of all its great heroes and allies.

This room also has the power to project great wealth onto any person in existence, so you take a mighty leap onto a hundred foot tall pile of gold coins and shout "Give great wealth to me on Earth!" There is a surge of power as the wish is granted. You take your time here, playing with some of your favorite items and admiring others.

Feeling wonderful, you run back up the illuminated staircase into the room of luck, and touch the giant star once again, mentally moving it back into place and closing the secret trapdoor beneath it. You pull ten, twenty sided dice from your pocket, and toss them on the ground. They all roll a 20, and you smile to yourself. You then take a short walk to the teleport circle and state: "Room of Great Knowledge."

In a flash you find yourself standing in a large circular chamber located in the northeast tower of the great castle. The walls are covered in magnificent one hundred foot high bookcases made of beautiful polished wood that are filled to the brim with books and digital files of all sizes.

At the entrance to the room is the mighty book of knowledge that resides in a glowing protective display case. Many great stories have been told around this mighty book. . In the center of the room is the most powerful computer ever created. It stands on a silver desk and is constantly being updated and made more powerful by a team of dedicated and gifted scientists and other super computers that stop at nothing to make the master computer ever improving.

The computer screen is a fifty feet by fifty feet and consists of a 3d holographic image that has perfect clarity. The computer has the ability to read your thoughts and can bring up the information to anything you are looking for instantly. The computer also has access to all of the knowledge and all of the greatest minds that have ever existed. It also has all of the greatest video games of all time, where even more heroes for Immortaland can be created.

You walk up to the computer and are greeted to a cheery "Hello Master, how may I serve you?" You think in your head of a problem that has been bothering you. There is a quick whir and the answer to the problem is projected onto the holograph screen.

You smile, then wave at one of the over hundred librarians that man this great fountain of knowledge. The librarians wave back, then get back to work collecting and organizing the various pieces of knowledge that have come through one of the many small magical portals.

Next to the computer is a specially designed super chair that has been programmed and designed by the universe's greatest minds for self-improvement exercises through brain-mind technology. You sit in the chair, and instantly feel like a complete genius. The chair has the power to increase your intellect one hundred fold, as well as permanently improve you in any aspect of life that you wish to be better at. You soak up the knowledge of the universe and smile, realizing nothing can stop you now. You feel limitless.

After a while you feel the need for some fun. You walk over to the flaming orange teleport circle and state: "Realm within a Realm." You suddenly find yourself in one of the most enjoyable parts of the castle. In this alternate reality you are all powerful. Anything you want to happen will happen. You can create anything you want from thin air just by thinking about it. There is no limit to your power here.

This room is as big as your imagination, a paradise within a paradise. There are hundreds of castles located throughout the land, filled with happy people, great heroes and heroines, kings and queens. You are their creator, and some like to worship you.

There are thousands of fabulous churches here, where the happy people come and give thanks for their perfect lives. Everything is as it should be here. There is no disease, no pollution, no crime, the weather is always incredible, businesses thrive, and everybody is happy.

Smiling, you jump into the air, summon your angelic wings, and fly to one of your many favorite churches. You magically appear in front of thirty people who are praying. They rejoice to see you, bright smiles on their faces as they cheer. You wave your hands, casting a powerful spell to heal them all to full strength. They then jump for joy when you throw diamonds, gold coins, and jewels to them. You wave to them and then teleport outside the church.

You fly to the nearby pleasure dome. This is a large dome the size of five football fields, made of enchanted stones and gems of all colors. There is no entrance save for one large golden door at the eastern base. It is guarded by two diamond statues of huge breasted Valkyries holding very large swords. The statues can come to life and will protect the pleasure dome to the end.

You fly up to the golden doors and then phase through them. You are instantly overcome with powerful pleasurable feelings. This room is filled with the most beautiful women of all the land. The women rush over to you, kissing you and covering you with sweet smelling aphrodisiac oils.

You feel the raw power of Love, and you let it flow through and around you. The incredible joy and ecstasy you feel is hard to describe, you are filled to overflowing with joy and pleasurable feelings. You spend many hours here, enjoying the millions of ways to find pleasure. Any fantasy can come true here, and often does. After fulfilling one last incredible fantasy, you leave the pleasure dome and head for the great hall of gaming.

Only one mile from the pleasure dome is the great gaming hall. This is a massive arena designed with a clever mix of magic and technology. Any game in the universe can be found here, and any player in the universe can be summoned here to play games with you.

Any game in existence can be played here, plus anything else the imagination can think up. In the center of the arena is a large oak table. Around the table are fifty leather chairs, studded in diamonds. Just by touching the table, your adrenaline starts to race and your competitive juices start to flow. It is also known that when you sit here, you are an unstoppable gaming machine with incredible intelligence, perception, skill, and reflexes. You walk over and sit at the table. A sly grin comes to your face as you state: "It's noob pwning time!"

You play several of your favorite games, relishing in the thrill of victory. You then play several other games located throughout the arena, sharpening your skills. After several fun filled hours you leave the gaming arena and teleport back to the throne room.

Your eyes immediately slide to a diamond bell next to the throne. This is the wartime bell, a powerful and ancient artifact. By ringing this bell you will send out a loud warning ring throughout Immortaland, alerting all of its occupants about some problem or emergency. The inhabitants will then all band together to solve the problem as quickly, efficiently, and intelligently as possible.

You smile, then touch the mighty gem of ultimate power in the center of the chamber and state boldly: "I want all that has happened while I have been here in Immortaland to come true to the best of all abilities!" There is a blast of power that bursts from the ultimate orb of power and out into the universe. You smile brightly as Genie appears at your side. Simultaneously Genie and the orb state: "Wish Granted, Anything else Great Master?" "Yes!" you state loudly, waving your arm and summoning your angelic wings, "Lets get to work making Immortaland even better than it was yesterday."

Some of the other powerful rooms and abilities of Immortaland are as follows:

Room of Writing and Creation: Nestled in a mighty chamber in the top half of the northwest tower of the castle lies one of the mightiest chambers in all of Immortaland.

You say the magic words: "Immortaland, Immortaland, Immortaland"

There is a flash, and then you find yourself standing in a magnificent circle of molten gems that sends sparkling light throughout a massive room of unlimited power. You find yourself in the mighty room of fantasy writing creation, where time and space have been mastered and twisted to the ultimate benefit of all who come here.

The eastern corner of this room is covered in a mighty thirty foot wide fireplace that glows with a magical orange fire. When you look closely at the hypnotic flames, all sorts of incredible ideas spring to your mind. The fireplace itself is made of polished rocks and cut gems, with mortar made of liquid amethyst that glows with a warm purple light. On top of the fireplace is a golden mantle that is covered with a wide assortment of trophies and awards.

The ceiling is fifty feet high and consists of a fantastic miniature universe that draws the beneficial energies from a billion other universes, and then transmits that energy at the optimum levels needed for creative thinking in a magical wave of light that shines from the various stars that twinkle in the ceiling sky.

All throughout this massive chamber there are multi-colored glowing orbs of creative energy. These orbs have magical powers that imbue all who enter here with incredible energy, incredible health and vitality, incredible powers of concentration, and incredible communicative powers. These orbs help turn thoughts and ideas into eloquent words and phrases in the most entertaining and dynamic ways possible.

Scattered throughout the room are desks, writing areas, and writing devices of all types. There are large slabs of polished crystals to write on, the greatest of all writing stations, desks of gold, ancient scrolls of power, and a most wondrous of machines that has the ability to transfer the greatest of thoughts into the most eloquent of phrases instantly.

In the western corner of this chamber is the greatest creative zone in all of space and time. With just the power of your mind, you can create any item, spell, effect, fantasy, feeling, world, person, or anything else desired for your ultimate enjoyment and anyone else you wish to share it with.

In front of the great fireplace is a finely woven magical flying carpet. It has the power to bring your mind to any fantasy that you choose to have, and make it as real as you want it to be. On the southern wall is a collection of computer images and life like reproductions of the cutest of small children, all begging for you to make Immortaland even better.

Next to the children are various heroes and other important people who work diligently in this chamber to come up with all sorts of ideas, inventions, and books. Whenever you enter this room, you love to write more fabulous stories and come up with even better ideas to better the universes.

On a mighty pedestal made of polished red and yellow streaked meteorite, there lies a glowing sphere of untold power. This sphere allows the user to get an instant power up to maximum strength, health, vitality, intelligence, emotional well-being, physical energy, or any other beneficial ability or feeling desired.

This power source can be used by any character in the kingdom at any time needed for the defense or improvement of Immortaland. You, of course, have unlimited usage. The mighty orb of power also has the ability to warp time. At will, time can be split, twisted, multiplied, speed up, slowed down, or manipulated in any way imaginable. Great fantasy or scientific creations, that may have taken centuries to produce or come up with, are now available in seconds or minutes due to the incredible powers of time twisting.

On the northern wall is a luxurious reclining chair that is hooked up to a magic portal of entertainment. The entertainment portal delivers incredible sound, a magic viewing screen of perfect clarity, and it induces a feeling of utter joy and happiness. The viewing screen can expand or shrink to any size or shape desired, even surrounding the user in a 3d world. The greatest of stories and tales can be accessed instantly, and played out in a stunning visual universe, maxed out in all ways possible for ultimate enjoyment.

Any scene or story can be played out as it actually happened, or it can be portrayed as the user wants it to be seen. The greatest of sounds, music, movies, shows, and events can be shown here, anything imaginable, or anything that has ever happened or been imagined can be seen. Any video game or videogame type experience can be played here with no limits, with the station being able to multiply itself as many times as needed for as many users as needed.

Next to the chair is a magical six inch tall fairy that will give you any number of magical treats at your command. These goodies will boost your energy and creativity levels, as well as your desire to work hard on your desired projects.

Another powerful ability of this room is for the user to be able to summon any person or sentient being that has ever lived to appear before them in astral form. You will then be able to talk and interact with them, as well as having the option of absorbing their beneficial characteristics, knowledge, and creative abilities.

This room is so powerful, that once even conceived, it will continue to get stronger and stronger. Once in this chamber, the occupant finds themselves divinely inspired, and their writings and creations come quickly and easily, magically transcribed for them. The books and projects that you create while in this chamber will fill the history books and computer data banks of all your great accomplishments for all of eternity.

Garden of Forgiveness: Nestled near the southwest tower is a beautiful flower garden. The flowers here are always in bloom, and their sweet scent is intoxicating. Throughout the garden are glowing statues of children, animals, heroes, and magical symbols. If you are feeling weighed down by negative thoughts or energy that needs to be released, this is the place to go.

All you need to do is enter or teleport into the garden and stroll through it. With each step, all past resentments and anger will be magically healed. While this is happening, the statues will begin to glow as bright as the sun, burning away the negative thoughts and energy. At the same time, the flowers will grow larger, absorbing the dark thoughts, and then explode in a fireworks display of positive energy. For every flower that explodes in pure healing power, more will spring from the ground to take its place.

Thirty feet in the air above the garden of forgiveness is a swirling purple whirlpool that sucks up all the negative energy in the area, bringing it to another dimension for cleansing and allowing pure holy goodness to replace the negative thoughts and energy.

The longer you spend time here, the more powerful the effect becomes, until all the negative energy and thoughts have been eliminated or transformed, leaving only peace, tranquility, and a feeling that it is fun to forgive.

In the center of the garden is a giant fountain, known as the fountain of forgiveness. This magnificent fountain contains water blessed by thousands of priests, purified in the holiest of artifacts, and then given its magical properties from the holiest of demi-gods.

Bathing in the fountain fills you with an inner resolve to not allow actions of the past to hinder your joy of the present and the future. While here, you will find it very easy to maintain a sense of peace and love that permanently replaces negative energy and emotions with positive emotions like love, and inner harmony.

A single drink of water from this fountain will keep your thoughts pure for several months. The fountains water also nourishes all of the garden's flowers and plant life here, enhancing their forgiving magic tenfold.

Tower of Inner Drive and Motivation: This chamber is located in the bottom half of the northwest tower of the castle. It is easily noticeable by the intense energy that constantly swirls about it, like a massive electrical storm. In addition to the multi-colored lightning and energies that circle about constantly, one can hear a powerful chanting.

The chanting is recorded in time and space, and loops endlessly in varied forms. It is the chant of the most powerful shamans, priests, wizards, demi-gods, warriors, humans, heroes, and aliens that have ever existed, merged into one ultra-powerful chant of ultimate goodness that sends shivers down your spine and then makes you want to rush to accomplish all of your dreams and desires.

The entrance to the tower is a fifteen foot tall red door made of hardened steel. The good citizens of Immortaland can access the tower at any time, and when they do, they feel a tremendous feeling of hope and power envelope them.

Once inside the tower, the chanting is louder and its effects are multiplied one hundred fold. The inside of the tower looks different for each person. The tower searches the individuals mind and soul, then creates a miniature 3d universe and tells a tale or story in movie form that allows the person to see, in no uncertain terms, what needs to be done in order for them accomplish their goals and dreams.

The magic in this chamber also shows the dream being accomplished over and over again, customizing the mind for certain success. No matter how beaten down an ally of Immortaland may be, just fifteen minutes in the tower of inner drive and motivation will have them feeling like an unstoppable force of nature that nothing in the universes can stop or deny.

Tower Defenses of Immortaland: There are tens of thousands of towers scattered throughout Immortaland. Some of them are visible while others are not. Each tower is occupied by archers, priests, wizards, knights, heroes, soldiers, helpers, and the most devastating destructive weapons imaginable by fantasy and science merged together.

These towers also have the ability to clone themselves up to one billion trillion times if there is an attack, and those clones have that ability as well. Any attackers usually find that time has stopped and they are utterly destroyed or captured before they even know what happened.

Chamber of Immortality: This chamber is hidden in a secret location of Immortaland that can be accessed by any of the teleporters throughout the kingdom by true friends of Immortaland. This is a chamber of pure magic, with one hundred foot wide walls and a two hundred foot high ceiling that swirl with every color of the rainbow.

Once in this chamber, you can eliminate any and all aging desired, and you can return to any age you wish, while keeping any knowledge, strength, ability, wisdom, etc. that you have attained since your last visit.

This room also gives you the powerful ability to save your progress in life, just like a video game. At any time, you may return to any of your save points throughout all of space and time.

Some choose to ignore this ability, and others love to correct all their mistakes by living forward, then using the knowledge gained to go back in time to an earlier save point to play their life even better, then making another save point once everything has been accomplished to satisfaction.

Another favorite ability of this chamber is to allow any user to make a diary of their life. This diary will remain here forever, for others to access for the improvement of all of creation as a whole. The user can create anything they want here. Some choose to leave an autobiography along with many pictures of themselves. Others choose to leave knowledge and advice from their life's experiences.

Some choose to leave great ideas, others choose to leave dna and perfect reproductions of their brains so that they can be brought back to life at a later point in time. Some choose to do all these things and more, making their own personal existence and triumphs a true masterpiece that future generations love to come and access.

Other known powers of Immortaland: In order to ensure that Immortaland is the greatest fantasy kingdom to exist and that will ever exist, it has developed quite an array of special powers and abilities.

Besides all of its already documented powers and abilities, it can instantly incorporate any kingdom into itself as an ally or it can clone the other kingdom a million times as a minion of Immortaland, and use those cloned kingdoms along with a litany of other options, to destroy, capture, or incorporate that kingdom into Immortaland. All the cloned kingdoms will remain as permanent guardians of Immortaland.

Immortaland can also use its priests and sorcerers to cast a mighty charm spell that will instantly affect whole kingdoms and universes, forcing all forms of life and artificial life to become immediate friends and allies of Immortaland and fight for its cause.

Immortaland can also make infinite copies of itself, stop time, and exist as a full kingdom in the smallest of hiding places throughout all of space and time. The number of defenses and abilities of Immortaland are limitless, and just get better and better over time, as a bastion of goodness that lives on forever.

IMMORTALAND
The Greatest Fantasy Kingdom To Exist
And That Will Ever Exist

www.Immortaland.com

Preview of Towers:

Kelyk raced up the stone steps, a few strides ahead of his younger brother. With a shout of joy he jumped the last step to the top of the tower. It had long been abandoned, but was still a mighty fortification. His father had told him many bedtime stories of soldiers that defended towers like this to help keep their land free. Pretending he had a sword in his hand, he sparred with his brother, both of them laughing as they imagined themselves to be heroes fighting off enemy invaders.

As the years went by, Kelyk ended up in the army. He was strong, tenacious, and had a charming personality that allowed him to rise to the rank of captain in a relatively short period of time. One day his commanding officer came to him with a difficult mission. He was to secure the southern border; he was to be given five hundred warriors, two hundred archers, twenty war engineers, one hundred cavalry, fifty knights, one hundred workers, and ten thousand gold pieces. It was a dangerous mission. In fact, the last five commanders and their armies where slaughtered, with only a few escaping to tell the tale. Kelyk was immediately alarmed.

"Why are you sending me to my death?" he asked, exasperated. "Think of this as an opportunity," the old warrior replied in a gruff voice. "If you can find a way to secure the southern border you will be hailed as a hero, and likely promoted to the rank of general."

"A lot of good that will do me if I'm dead!" stated Kelyk defiantly, a sneer on his lips. "Easy soldier, remember what happens to those who disobey orders. Anyway, the king himself has sent you a secret weapon to help." Grizzletooth moved in close and whispered, "We have a wizard that is to join you." Kelyk took a step back, surprise evident on his face. "Really? What types of magic does he do? How powerful a wizard are we talking? Does he take orders from me?" Grizzletooth smiled, "Yes, he will take your commands, and as for his powers, you will have to ask him yourself."

Kelyk looked up into the bright blue sky and suddenly had a feeling of confidence, as he knew just how rare wizards where in the kingdom. "Ok, I'll do it! But tell the king I need fifty catapults as well. We will teach the barbarian scum once and for all to leave our kingdom in peace!"

Grizzletooth beamed with pride and gave Kelyk a hearty slap on the back. "Now you're talking soldier! I'll let the general know the good news and see if we can get those catapults for ya!"

A few days later the order came down. They were leaving in a week and Kelyk was to meet with the top general in one hour to go over the plans. He headed to his house to freshen up and put on his best suit of armor. As he is shaving in the mirror, his mind wanders back to his childhood, to a happier time when he and his brother would play among the old towers. A slight smile crossed his lips and then he straightened up and looked dead center into the mirror, his eyes steely and glinting. "That's it!" he shouts. "I will cover the southern borders with so many towers that the enemy will quake in fear and not dare to enter our territory again!" With a sense of purpose Kelyk polished his armor and made sure his longsword was razor sharp. He then headed outside and made his way to the castle.

The sun glinted off his silver armor as he jumped onto his faithful steed and galloped towards the king's mighty castle a little over a mile away. The guards at the gate immediately let him through, and within seconds a skinny page took his horse. The war room was located in the northeast tower. After passing through several security checkpoints, Kelyk soon found himself face-to-face with the mighty general. General Vyrak is an imposing figure, standing over six and a half feet tall and covered in scars and muscle. Kelyk has heard many tales of the general's exploits; he is a living legend. Kelyk salutes then states: "Reporting for duty."

General Vyrak glares at Kelyk, a burning fire in his eyes. In a voice deep, gruff, and dangerous the general states, "The southern border has become more than an embarrassment, it is now threatening the kingdom itself. Kelyk, the king's seer has predicted that you have the greatest chance for success. She has also predicted a great tragedy for our nation if you should fail."

Check out the rest of the story in book or audio book format on my website: www.LordHartRules.com

My Other Books and Audio Books

For A Special Treat, check out my
<u>AUDIO BOOKS</u>

Thanks for reading!

If you enjoyed this book a nice review would be greatly appreciated.

Check Out all My Books and Audio Books at:
www.LordHartRules.com